Shattered LIVES

JULIE FREEMAN

ISBN 979-8-88945-479-3 (softcover)
ISBN 979-8-88945-480-9 (ebook)

This is a work of fiction based on a true crime. Names, places and certain incidents are the product of the author's artistic expression. Any resemblance of actual locales, events-persons living or deceased-is purely coincidental.

Disclaimer: This book is based on some true events, however, names, characters, business, places, events identifying details and incidents have been fictionalized to protect the privacy of the individuals.

Printed in the United States of America.

Brilliant Books Literary
137 Forest Park Lane Thomasville
North Carolina 27360 USA

Contents

Foreword

The "domino effect" comes to mind, when I think about the people in this story whose lives tumbled down into a sequential chain reaction of turmoil and loss. Nothing in the lives of these people as they knew it before has remained intact. Prior to her daughter's murder, Laurel Colton was a successful special education teacher of 20 years, who worked tirelessly for students with developmental disorders. Today, she remains devastated by the loss of her daughter and has given up her love of teaching and her marriage of 40 years. Jillian Jackson has also given up the life that she once embraced as a successful real estate broker. Melanie Guilbeau still reminisces about the good times she had with her best friend. Old pictures of the two young, smiling school girls, once inseparable, adorn random pieces of quirky furniture throughout her apartment, but also serve as a painful reminder of the dark fiery night she lost her best friend to a senseless act of violence. And Donnie Jackson has outlived his 21-year-old- son, Collin. While many of the characters in this story have struggled to hold on to a blind faith, the ultimate act of murder forever altered and shattered many lives.

Note to Reader

This is a true crime account of a story based on fiction. In order to protect the identities of the innocent and remain ethical to those who were reluctant to publish their own personalized account of this story, the names, places, identifying characteristics and details such as physical properties, occupations, places of residence, and the events throughout this story have been altered.

Dedication

Writing is my passion and because of it, later in life I returned to Louisiana State University Manship School of Mass Communication where this story began as a term paper and a few years later emerged into a book upon the encouragement of Professor Jay L. Perkins, who served as a reporter, editor and political analyst for the Associated Press for 15 years, covering Capitol Hill and also serving as a writing consultant for the *Washington Times*. Among all of my outstanding journalism professors at the LSU Manship School, I credit him most in teaching me how to write.

Without the devotion of so many great mentors from the LSU Manship School Mass Communication and the support of my family, I could have not written this book. They encouraged me to be persistent and, with determination, I found Calvin Coolidge's omnipotence.

To my late mother in law, Mary Emerson Canning who was a force of nature, an avid reader, lover of poetry and was related to Ralph Waldo Emerson, I owe my deepest appreciation for her interest and honest reflection. I am thankful for providing me with a beautiful, quiet place to write this book at his cabin nestled in the serenity of the beautiful quiet nature of the woods.

To my son, Jake, I owe every missed opportunity away from him while in school studying journalism. May this book provide you with an example to always follow your passions and dreams in life, and remember, "It's not how many times you fall, but how many times you get up."

Finally, I owe my deepest gratitude to my beloved late father, Jim Freeman, who left this world way too soon, but while here, taught me the value of hard work and to always reach for the stars. In my heart, I know that he is a part of that great constellation up above shining down on me each night.

Thou Shalt Not Kill
Exodus 20:14

Donnie Jackson panicked. He felt threatened. He wanted to leave, but the old blue pick-up truck stalled while the little boy seated next to him pleaded with him not to leave his side.

As the first shot rang out and pierced Diana Jackson's chest, she stumbled backwards.

The menacing power of the shooter's 9mm semi-automatic pistol fired off three more shots in machine gun-like action striking Diana a second time in the back. As her body fell to the ground, her face took on an expression of shock and disbelief. The little boy jumped out of his father's truck and ran to his mother, clinging to her as she lay dying in a pool of blood. His hands trembling, Donnie turned the gun on himself and fired a shot through his stomach, tearing a hole through his liver and shattering his spleen.

Within minutes of the shootings, off-duty Deputy Sheriff Harry O'Conner, was dispatched to the massive scene of blue flashing emergency lights and the piercing sounds of police and ambulance sirens, flanked by a crowd of curious on- lookers at a new popular night spot, Pascals, that O'Connor often referred to as "that damn watering hole." At least one night of the week, O'Conner found himself breaking up a fight between belligerent drunks who were regulars at the crowded, smoke-filled bar.

As police officers descended upon the wounded man lying on the ground, O'Conner looked down to find his old high school buddy, Donnie Jackson, writhing in pain from a gaping self-inflicted gunshot wound, yelling, "Shoot me! Shoot me, Harry!" But Harry O'Connor would not shoot him. As crowds of people continued to gravitate towards the maelstrom of a sea of bewildered bystanders staring at the crazed man smeared in blood mumbling incoherent epithets while carried off in an ambulance. All that remained to be seen in the darkness of night was the yellow police crime scene tape illuminated by the parking lot post lights, where a small petite woman in her late 20's lie face down in a pool of blood.

Quiet, sullen and insulated by shock, Melanie Guilbeau, walked in a zombie-like state holding the dead woman's child past the crime scene tape and knelt down beside her friend's lifeless body, wiping the blood off her face before she was gently led away by police officers.

Later at the police station while Melanie identified Donnie Jackson as Diana's killer, veteran homicide Detective Phillip Jarreau struggled to maintain his composure as the dead woman's 5-year-old little boy asked, "Is my mommy going to die?" He then looked down at his hands covered in his mother's blood and said with a smile, "It must be cheesecake."

Hours later, while Donnie lay in a hospital bed like a soldier mortally wounded in combat, Diana lay lifeless, her jet black hair matted, messy and saturated in blood. Doctors and nurses fought desperately to save her life, but the pupils of her eyes remained fixed and dilated, and doctors could find no blood pressure or carotid pulse. Her heart was flaccid and in a state of relaxation, destitute of any blood. She was officially pronounced dead 25 minutes after midnight.

Donnie

Donovan Edwin Jackson, III grew up in a loving upper middle-class family in Baton Rouge, Louisiana.

Baton Rouge is located in the southeast portion of the state of Louisiana along the Mississippi River where the summers are hot, humid and pre-disposed to tornadic activity yearlong. It is a major petrochemical center of the American South. A building boom began in the 1990's with new construction happening all over the city.

Donnie Jackson was one of two children from the union of Dale and Jillian Jackson. He and his brother, Matthew, often referred to as "Mattie" were identical twins. "School came easy to me, but I was the introvert and had few friends, unlike Donnie, who hated school and was the extrovert—always surrounded by a group of friends creating a scene of raucous laughter," explained Mattie.

"I could not have asked for a better friend in good times and in bad," recounted Donnie's long-time friend, Brett Salsbury.

He was also well-liked by the girls.

Tiffany Richie, Donnie's first love, gushed about him.

"It was love at first sight. Donnie was always a loving, giving and caring individual. I will always hold a special place for him in my heart. He would always try to go out of his way to help anybody he could."

At first glance, teachers could not tell Donnie and Mattie apart, but their distinctive personalities always gave away their separate identities. Donnie was the mischievous one always playing pranks while Mattie's eyes remained transfixed on the blackboard. "When I graduated from high school with a 4.0. and Donnie barely managed a 2.0. in order to graduate, he felt really dumb." But Mattie insisted he was just as smart as him, but just didn't like school. Nevertheless, at the age of sixteen, Donnie had a charismatic charm about him with teachers and students alike.

But, the sweet sixteen-year-old boy started hanging out with the wrong crowd and was using drugs.

"I was 16 years old when I started using and used until I was 33 years old. Drugs were my downfall," Donnie would later recall. While Donnie and Mattie would always remain close, as adults they began to look more like distant cousins than identical twins. Donnie was taller and more muscular with darker hair than Mattie, and gave off of a devil-may-care attitude in contrast to Mattie's reserved demeanor. After high school, Donnie joined his father's construction company, while Mattie went off to college to pursue a civil engineering degree.

While Donnie was privileged to be grandfathered into one of the family businesses, his father Dale Jackson was a no-nonsense man with an entrepreneurial spirit who not only managed a successful construction company but also owned a number of rental properties that he expected his son to independently manage without the headache of dealing with unreliable subcontractors for the ongoing maintenance and the upkeep of his properties' jobs such as plumbing that he could do for himself.

But Donnie proved to be more unreliable than the subcontractors Dale Jackson would have hired to keep his properties intact and business running smoothly. Tenants would often call Dale Jackson's house at all hours of the night complaining about faulty sinks, toilets, and a host of other problems that were supposed to be taken care of weeks, sometimes months ago, as promised by Donnie. Even worse, Dale Jackson discovered his son wasn't performing credit checks on prospective renters with risky credit histories. Instead of collecting rental payments, Dale Jackson found himself preoccupied with preparing eviction notices. In some cases, unbeknownst to Dale, Donnie had simply pocketed the money, and tenants became belligerent and outraged when they learned they were being evicted, insisting they had made their monthly rental payments. Dale Jackson found himself cleaning up a hell of a mess while Jillian tried to allay her husband's concerns attributing their son's lack of responsibility to a lack of business experience. She also insisted Dale increase Donnie's salary. Who could live on that kind of meager salary and make ends meet, she protested. As always, Dale gave in to his beloved wife's wishes and agreed to give Donnie a second chance, but not without a long list of stipulations. Even so, things didn't improve and Dale was continuing to lose money while Donnie became increasingly unreliable, spending more time at the local bars than managing the family business. Pascals became his favorite haunt and cocaine his favorite drug.

Donnie and Diana

On a hot humid summer night while having beers at his regular hang-out, a striking brunette, Diana Colton, walked in and caught Donnie's eye. He wasted no time in pursuing her. The attraction was mutual, instantaneous and they quickly fell for each other and became an item. It didn't matter that when Donnie met Diana she had a two-week old baby. He fell head-over-heels in love with both of them. After a brief courtship, on Sept. 2, 1985, the couple announced they were getting married, and also expecting a child. It was a surprise for Donnie's family, but his mother, Jillian, welcomed both Diana and her baby girl, Keeley, to the family with open arms.

On June 3, 1986, Collin Donovan Jackson came into the world and completed Donnie and Diana's family.

The couple settled into family life in a small apartment in south Baton Rouge, and to Dale Jackson's relief, married life seemed to have transformed his son into a changed man. Gone were the days of bar-hopping and blowing money, and Donnie began to work hard at Jackson & Klein Construction proving himself to be reliable and accountable, effectively assisting his father with the day-to-day operations of the family businesses. But, after the birth of Collin, Diana became increasingly homesick and longed to return home to be near her family in Covington. Without any formal education or job prospects, Donnie abruptly left the family business behind and eventually found work that paid half of what he was earning with his father's construction company at a small business in New Orleans where the young family of four moved into a tiny apartment in the French Quarter on Baronne Street.

Founded by the French and spiced up by the Spanish, New Orleans is the birthplace of jazz and some of the world's most popular musicians—from Fatz Domino to Lenny Kravitz—where people from all over the world come to embellish in the debauchery of this exotic city often referred to as the "Big Easy".

Here in this mystical part of the American south, is a melting pot of French, Spanish and Caribbean influences.

On any given night, the sounds of Jazz, high energy music and symphonies stream out into the cobblestone streets of the French Quarter. Central to Jackson Square, is the heart of the French Quarter, shrouded with tourists, hip artists, voodoo museums and historical buildings and homes overlooking the Mississippi River where a steady stream of cargo ships travel on a daily basis transporting raw materials.

Celebratory festivals are commonplace to New Orleans where a way of life began centuries ago with the French saying, "Laissez Le Bons Temps Rouler"- Let the Good times Roll! And on every year between February and March, Mardi Gras celebrations begin with an unprecedented number of tourists from all over the world who travel to participate in the Carnival festivities. Masked Krewes and celebrities flanked in purple green and gold, who represent New Orleans' elite social organizations roll down the mystical streets of the French Quarter in elaborate, decorative floats, among scores of bead-hungry crowds of tourists, yelling "throw me something mista!" The streets are wild with intoxication, where it is not uncommon for female tourists to flash their breasts to a rowdy crowd for the sake of plastic purple and gold beads.

About 45 minutes from the city of New Orleans is the city of Covington, a small Southern close knit community surrounded by twisted oak trees and three beautiful rivers. Its historic downtown is lined with fine art galleries and a mix of boutiques. Seemingly a world away from the bustling Big Easy, the town is a small, friendly community surrounded by scenic views of bayous, rivers, parks and quiet charming residential communities where Stan and Laurel Colton chose to start their lives together and raise a family.

Stan and Laurel met in college at Louisiana Tech in Ruston, Louisiana, where both graduated with high honors. After Laurel received a degree in special education and Stan was accepted into law school, the lovebirds decided to elope before Stan began law school. It was a disappointment to Laurel's mother, who always envisioned a large elaborate wedding for her only daughter, but in time she got over it and the newlyweds had their marriage blessed at St. Mary's Catholic Church in Covington followed by a swanky reception for the new bride and groom at the posh Windsor Court Hotel in New Orleans.

After a brief honeymoon in the Big Easy, Laurel accepted a position at Covington Elementary School, where she won the respect and appreciation of students and teachers alike as an outstanding teacher, who had seemingly unstoppable energy and the patience of Job, but lately she seemed tired, and after a routine visit to her doctor, she discovered she was pregnant. While she was thrilled with the news of having a baby, her husband didn't seem as enthusiastic. After all, he had barely finished his first year of law school and finances were tight.

On the strike of midnight marking the advent of the New Year of 1960 Laurel gave birth to Dalton Stanley Colton. A second baby, Danya Kate Colton soon followed not long after her firstborn. By then, Stan had passed the bar exam and accepted a position with a prominent law firm in New Orleans and the couple settled into a two-story classic southern home on 1934 Oak Knoll Street, lined with century old oaks and sprawling ranch style homes with their two children. As Stan became more successful in his law practice and earned a partnership, he encouraged Laurel to quit her job and stay home with the children, but Laurel felt a sense of duty to her students who she believed were faced with extraordinary challenges, and continued to teach. However, not long after the Colton family had settled in their new home on Oak Knoll Street, Laurel discovered she was pregnant again. Since neither Stan or Laurel planned on having any more children, Stan was surprised and Laurel in shock.

She cried throughout her entire pregnancy and seemed inconsolable. She was not prepared to be up all night with another baby. Dalton and Danya were just getting old enough to go to school and she was not ready to start over she tearfully confessed to her childhood priest at St. Mary's Catholic Church. He assured her everything would be just fine and that the baby would bring her and her family much joy. He was right.

On April 9, 1964, Diana Joy Colton joined the Colton family. She was a beautiful baby with big blue eyes, fine angelic facial features and thick, jet black hair. She was a happy baby that rarely cried and slept wonderfully like an angel throughout the night.

As a toddler she walked and talked earlier than the other children. As a little girl, she loved to dance and did so until the last day of her life.

Diana was every parent's wish. She was beautiful, smart, talented and full of potential. In high school, she was the captain of the dance team and graduated as high school valedictorian with a 4.0. grade point average. After high school, like her parents, she chose Louisiana Tech and majored in music and dance. After earning a degree in Music and Dramatic Arts, she moved to Baton Rouge and opened a dance studio with her best friend from high school, Melanie Guilbeau. "Diana had it all," Melanie said. She always had a date and life was really going her way. She purchased a nice little bungalow home nestled in a maturely landscaped neighborhood in the popular southern garden district that she creatively remodeled with an originally carved stone gas-burning fireplace and updated the old washed up kitchen with maple wood cabinetry. She was as talented in her personal life as she was in her professional life. Each dance recital was painstakingly choreographed to the last minute detail by Diana with unbridled creativity. With each passing year, more students signed up to attend her dance classes. Her studio had become so popular she had a waiting list of little girls' parents who were desperate to grab a spot for their child on stage. With each passing year, Diana's choreography became more innovative and her tiny little dancers more talented and theatrical in performance.

As busy as her work schedule had become, Diana, like her mother with unstoppable energy, still somehow managed to maintain an active social life. Melanie recalled that she had her share of dates but was never too keen on the bar scene. But, on one hot summer night, Melanie convinced Diana to go out with her to a new popular night club, Pascal's where her fate would be sealed.

TOXIC LOVE

Laurel Colton didn't like Donnie Jackson from the day she met him. She instinctively did not trust him. His answers to her litany of questions were vague and his behavior peculiar. She suspected he was high on drugs or alcohol, and hardly a suitable partner for her daughter, but Dale had seen men come and go in Diana's life and none of them in Laurel's eyes were suitable for her beloved Diana. In reality, for all of Diana's good qualities, picking out men was not one of them. When Diana called home to tell her parents she was pregnant by a man that she had a brief tumultuous relationship with prior to meeting Donnie, they were devastated but eventually accepted it and Diana proved to be an exceptional single mother to her little girl, Keeley Elizabeth. But just as life seemed to have settled into a comfortable, stable life for her and her daughter, Donnie Jackson walked into Diana's life and the next call the Coltons received from their daughter announcing that she and Donnie were getting married and expecting a child, literally took Laurel's breath away. While preparing Stan's favorite pot roast in her newly renovated kitchen, she became light headed, her eyes blurry, her legs gave away on the newly installed Mexican tile kitchen floor.

For months the couple had been arguing. Donnie begged and pleaded with his estranged wife to come home, but it was too late. The couple's union was not meant to last and they were going through a bitter divorce. Diana's friends would say Donnie had a problem with cocaine and Donnie's friends would say Diana was an unfaithful, flirtatious wife. How Diana would have had the time to run around on her husband while caring for two children, managing a dance studio and helping out her mother-in- law with her office's financial affairs was questionable, but Jillian Jackson had been stuck in the middle of her son and his wife's troubles for so long that their marital problems had become a part of her daily life and whether voluntarily or reluctantly, she remained a daily fixture in the eye of their stormy relationship.

Donnie wanted his family more than anything. Diana wanted him, but didn't want him. As soon as he would start dating someone else, she wanted him to reconcile. She called him and said she wanted the family back together, and then changed her mind. She would come over to his apartment and start yelling and the manager said if he got another complaint, they were going to make him move.

As the war raged on between the couple, a time bomb was ticking and about to go off.

Jillian Jackson recalls the last phone conversation she had with her distraught son as if it were yesterday. "He was hysterical. He said, 'Mom this is torture. I can't take it anymore.'"

Diana's words to Donnie in the last phone conversation they would ever have drove a knife straight through his heart. She was having an affair with his best friend, and the knife dug deeper as his estranged wife described for him in detail how much better a lover his friend was to her.

Nightmare

On Aug. 10, 1991, Donnie Jackson spent the day with his son, Collin, at a friend's house working on his old blue pick-up truck. Later that evening, he invited more friends over to join them for a bar-be-cue.

Tall, muscular, and handsome, Donnie never had a problem attracting women. Since his marriage to Diana had crumbled, he wasted no time in finding a new girlfriend, Candice Myers. He was trying to move on with his life since his separation from Diana, but even though the marriage was over, the custody battle was not. Donnie had argued all day long with Diana. The arguing continued into the early evening at the bar-be-cue as a stream of calls rolled in to Donnie from Diana. She had become increasingly paranoid about the time Donnie spent with Collin. She believed he was still abusing drugs and fearful something terrible might happen to Collin on a weekend visitation. But despite all the contention, Donnie was in good spirits being with the little boy who seemingly idolized him. When it was Donnie's weekend to be with Collin, they went out for ice cream and spent time at the park. But on this particular weekend, he forgot to tell his girlfriend that he would have Collin and wouldn't be able to meet her at the new hot spot in town Pascals later that night as originally planned. After phoning her several times, without receiving an answer, he hopped into his pickup truck with the little boy who was never two steps behind him, and drove to the popular night club to leave a note on Candace's car.

Around 11:30 p.m. Donnie Jackson arrived at Pascal's around the same time his estranged wife and her friend, Melanie Guilbeau, were exiting the lounge into the parking lot. Seeing Donnie with her son there at such a late hour made Diana furious. Diana ran ahead and approached Donnie's truck and chastised her estranged husband for having her son out so late.

Melanie caught up with Diana and pleaded with her friend to leave.

"Please, Diana, let's just leave."

But, Diana refused. She pulled away and told her, "I appreciate what you're doing, but you don't understand."

Diana then told her friend to call the police. She wanted her child.

Collin Jackson's nightmare was real. He watched in horror as gun shots were fired and his mother fell to the ground. He heard two more shots and saw his father lying on the ground only a few feet away from his mother.

Drugged Monster

At Donnie Jackson's trial the power-hungry prosecutor Trenton Calloway ripped into his opening statement and described the crime to the jury as a cowardly despicable execution, and attacked the defendant's theory of the case.

"As far as intoxication, the fact of an intoxicated or drugged condition of the defendant at the time of the commission of the crime is immaterial. If you're out in a bar and somebody drops a powerful drug in your drink but you don't know it, and you drink it and you don't know you're in the United States of America and you turn into a monster, sure you are exempted. You didn't voluntarily take that drug. In a nutshell, you can't go out and get drugged up and kill somebody and asked to be excused!"

Then the state called witnesses to the stand to testify against Donnie's longstanding threat to kill Diana.

Diana's step-sister, Tammy Tasson, testified to the jury that she overhead Donnie make several threats to kill Diana.

"He said, if I can't have you, no one else will have you," she testified to the jury.

Other state witnesses testified that at various times in the past Donnie had threatened to kill Diana due to their marital problems and the ongoing custody battle of Collin, but no one ever took those threats seriously. It was a bitter divorce and friends and family often heard both Diana and Donnie threaten each other.

Trenton Calloway moved the trial swiftly along in a courtroom show down. He hammered away about Diana Colton Jackson's life and how much she had to live for. In high school she was captain of the dance team, an honor student, graduated as high school valedictorian and then went on to college and graduated from Louisiana Tech. Afterwards, she opened a successful dance studio where she taught children to dance.

What he didn't mention to the jury was Jillian's claim that her daughter-in-law had stolen approximately $40,000 from her. "I trusted her like my own daughter and gave her complete control to oversee my business' financial and accounting affairs," said Jackson.

The jury also didn't hear about Jillian's claims of Diana 's extramarital affairs, and how she would leave the office in the presence of her mother- in-law, to be with other men, and not return for hours.

"I would watch her leave at lunch time and get into cars with different men in the parking lot. She would come back hours later with her hair and make-up looking like a hot mess," recounted Jillian.

In Jillian Jackson's mind, the jury would not hear the whole story. They would not hear about Diana 's moral character and her alleged infidelities that might influence their decision-making process in preponderance of the evidence and facts and circumstances of the case, in order to reach a verdict that would alter so many lives.

Donnie Jackson and his family hoped and prayed that the jury would have mercy and find him guilty of manslaughter, but after closing arguments, the jury deliberated for three hours and found him guilty of second degree murder.

Model Prisoner

Donnie Jackson has served fifteen years of his life at Louisiana State Penitentiary in Angola, Louisiana.

Angola is located at the base of the Tunica hills in a beautiful scenic region of Louisiana. The prison is situated on the land of a former plantation and slave breeding ground, with individual camps containing sleeping and recreational quarters fenced in by the hills and the Mississippi River.

Jackson is now 50 years old and no longer the young fit man with thick dark brown hair he once sported in his prime. Today, he is a soft-spoken, moderately overweight middle-aged man with thinning salt and pepper grey hair, who resembles a friendly neighbor or church member, and hardly a convicted killer.

Under a daily security guard's watch, Jackson has lived among approximately 70 other convicted felons in an individual camp. But, this is not a "camp" in the traditional sense of the word. It is prison where most inmates die and never go home. Here, silence, peace and quiet are rare. It is a sweat-box or ice-box, depending on the season— always rampant with perpetual noise and commotion. Inmates are always seeking control over other inmates. It's a power struggle.

It is a place where a man not only loses his freedom, but his privacy and dignity. Inmates share the shower facilities and toilets. Nothing is sacred. Everyday luxuries such as air conditioning are non-existent. The inmates are required to wake up at 5:00 a.m. and work all day in the Louisiana heat planting tomatoes or picking field peas while closely supervised by guards riding horseback with shotguns. One wrong move and you're a dead man.

But, through it all, Donnie's deep faith has kept him strong.

"There is only one way that I have been able to make it all this time. I have stayed close to God, going to church, praying and doing for others. I am a servant of the Lord. I keep trusting him."

Through hard work and dedication, life behind bars has paid off in some ways for Jackson. He no longer chooses drugs, but Jesus. He has worked hard to rehabilitate himself through spiritual activities and other self-improvement classes.

His model prison record has enabled him to work as a prison trustee who has helped care for and train prison guard dogs, and cook meals for the warden at the prison ranch house. He has also worked as a trustee in the prison tool shop.

This is the most freedom that Donnie may ever have.

A Mother's Love

Jillian Jackson is an age-defying 70-year-old woman who could easily pass for 50. She is a dark-haired timeless beauty with a dazzling smile. Her dark deep brown eyes light up one minute and blink back tears the next when she talks about her imprisoned son. But, with unstoppable energy and enthusiasm, she is always focused on her family while running a successful real estate business that has been in existence for 40 years. The burning scented candles in her office emanate a sense of warmth, complimented by photos of her children, grandchildren and great grandchildren scattered about the walls and furniture of her office. Her face lights up when she talks about her family. She has zealously stuck by her son and never misses an opportunity to visit him.

She talks about her next visit to see him behind the walls of prison as if she were going on a vacation.

"It's Donnie's 50th birthday so I am baking a cake cooking dinner, we are going to celebrate his birthday next weekend," she says enthusiastically.

But, Jillian Jackson is a broken woman. Her smile quickly fades, her voice cracks and she breaks down as she recalls seeing her son after he was sentenced to a life in prison.

"When I went to see him, I did not recognize him when he started walking towards me. He had gained 40 pounds. He walked right up to me and said, 'Mom, are you going to hug and kiss me?' Aren't you glad to see me?' You never think as a mother that a day would come that you would not recognize your own son. He told me he didn't want to live."

Donnie Jackson's mother is also a woman of faith and courage. She is motivated by an extraordinary maternal love for her son that only a mother can understand within the depths of her heart. "I have faithfully visited Donnie every possible moment I could even when my heart was so heavy and painful knowing I had to leave him there. I am slowly realizing that as my life continues and I am facing my own mortality that my life will not be complete until Donnie is home. My prayer has been for Donnie to come home while I am still alive so I can see my son and his family together once again."

No Mercy

On Dec. 15, 2007, it seemed Jillian Jackson's prayers had been answered. The Louisiana Board of Pardons voted unanimously for her son's early release.

On December 20, 2007, three days before Christmas, Pardon Board Chairman Evan Foxx sent a letter to East Baton Rouge Parish District Attorney, Dave Moreno, to inform him of the board's decision for recommendation of a commuted sentence for Donnie Jackson.

Fifteen years ago, a five-year-old boy was pleading with his father not to leave his side. Time nor circumstances had not changed that. Now 21, Collin Jackson stood before the twelve members of the pardon board, pleading for his father's early release. Overcome with emotion, he tearfully defended his father's actions. He told board members his father was struggling with drugs and alcohol at the time of the shooting and that he was not in his right mind.

In one of his many letters addressed to the board, he tried in vein to explain his father's actions. "It was not my father who killed my mom, it was drugs. I know my Dad is sorry for what he did. I would appreciate y'all giving my Dad a chance to come home and be with me. I need and love my Dad very much."

Collin's plea was also supported in a letter by Diana's mother, Laurel Colton, who remains devastated by the man who took her daughter's life, but has found peace through forgiveness.

"I've suffered a great loss when Donnie decided to take my daughter's life, but thanks to God and a few family members and friends, I have done a lot of healing. I no longer have all the anger and hatred for Donnie."

In further support, friends and family of Donnie Jackson rallied together and wrote 280 letters to Governor Bill Carlyle in support of his early release.

Others weren't so forgiving, and contested it.

Diana Jackson's best friend Melanie Guilbeau who witnessed her friend's murder was in opposition.

Guilbeau appeared on television and said, "Diana 's dying wish was that Donnie remain in prison for the rest of his life," even though her statement was never made at trial.

The officer at the scene of the crime Deputy Sheriff Harry O'Connor also joined the media circus, and allegedly embellished his trial testimony.

"He shot her in the back like a rabbit dog and was laughing and said, 'is she dead yet,'" recounted Jillian Jackson as she watched in disbelief as local television stations aired these people's lies.

Then District Attorney, Dave Moreno, hammered the final nail in the coffin.

"There is no excuse for his criminal conduct," Moreno wrote. "He gave no mercy to his victim. He should serve his life sentence in its entirety."

Three days before Christmas, the governor rejected the board's recommendation to commute Donnie Jackson's sentence.

"The governor reached the decision based on information that was not available to the Pardon Board prior to making its recommendation," said Nancy Gautreau, Moreno's press secretary. When asked what new information the governor received, Gautreau said she could not elaborate.

Today, Jillian Jackson is devastated, but still strong with determination and driven by an inexplicable hope, that she will someday bring her son home. "My son's life is in your hands at this point. I hope and pray that God will touch your heart. Please read this letter and reconsider changing your denial of his pardon," she carefully writes in perfect penmanship to the governor.

On January 15, 2003, Donnie Jackson appealed to the Fifth Circuit Court of Appeal but on March 30, 2004, Jackson's appeal was denied.

Collin Jackson is a sad, troubled young man devastated about the governor's decision.

"I really need my father. I've had a hard life without him," he writes in a heartfelt plea letter to the governor.

Just like the little boy who was always a step behind the father he idolized, now 21, Collin follows in his father's footsteps, walking down the same path of desperation, leading to alcohol and drugs.

Black Christmas

On a cold December night in 2009 as Jill Jackson added the last string of Christmas lights to her Christmas tree, she looked out her window and saw the familiar blue flashing lights of a police car. As she watched the police officeer walk towards her front door, she wasn't alarmed. After all, it wasn't unusual for the police to be called out to her neighbors' house in the middle of the night. Larry and Sheila Roberts had resided in the two-story stately blue home adjacent to the Jacksons for 20 years and often got into spats after a few too many cocktails. An argument would inevitably ensue and police would be called, but it was usually resolved in a short manner of time. Sometimes Sheila would leave the family home to stay the night with Jillian and Dale, or her husband would leave to stay the night with his brother who lived a few blocks away.

As Jillian Jackson opened her front door for the police officer, she laughed at the sight of her new fresh Christmas wreath fall into the hands of the officer. She welcomed him inside the warmth of her home that smelled of cinnamon candles and the fresh pine scent of a newly cut Christmas tree. She offered him a fresh cup of hot chocolate as she added another log to the fireplace. She would tell him she had seen nor heard nothing of the ruckus next door and return to the comfort of her favorite easy chair to admire the twinkling lights glistening on the large freshly cut Christmas tree adorned with an array of sentimental holiday ornaments. But, as she studied the stoic police officer's face standing before her, a sick wave of nausea overcame her and she knew something was terribly wrong.

Growing up without a mother or father, Jillian and Dale Jackson had tried to raise Collin well, but he proved to be more than they could handle in their elderly years. He floated back and forth between Diana's parents' home and Jillian and Dale's home, while his drug problem had become ever increasingly worse. Despite spending thousands of dollars on psychiatrists and the best rehabilitation clinics, after a brief stint in one of many intensive in-patient facilities, Collin remained clean for a short period and then went back to his old ways of using drugs. Days would turn into weeks before they would hear from him and when they did, it was always for money. Dale would flatly refuse his requests and Jillian would offer him to come home and join them for a nice home cooked meal. He would accept the invitation, but never without leaving with a handful of money that Jillian secretly gave to him while Dale wasn't looking.

Laurel Colton had grieved so much over her daughter's death, her grandson's drug problem wasn't as painful to her as his striking resemblance to her dead daughter. Collin had inherited his mother's thick black hair and fine facial features that had once landed him an ad in a popular men's magazine, but he wasn't interested in a modeling, but drugs. While Cocaine was once his father's drug of choice, Methamphetamine was Collin's drug of choice, and lately Diana's parents had become frightened to be around him. He had threatened them, stole from them and started to become violent towards them. They soon accepted the heartbreaking realization that they could no longer allow him to live with them or come and go as he pleased. Still, whether Jillian Jackson was the eternal optimist or in complete denial, she continued to empathize with Collin's dreadful plight in life and encouraged Dale to do the same. She reasoned with her grim-faced husband, bearing deep lines of fatigue etched in his face, that Collin had neither a mother or father. He needed them, she cried. Dale Jackson was for once unmoved. In 40 years of marriage Dale Jackson couldn't recall ever telling his wife "no." He had zealously stood behind her and supported her through it all. He had caved in to her every request for money that Collin used to support his drug habit, but as he moved closer to the age of retirement, he could no longer allow Collin to throw away the family's hard earned money. He knew he would finally have to take a firm stance against his wife.

As Jillian Jackson continued to study the police officer's face, she didn't sense that this had anything to do with her two drunk neighbors, nor did she sense Collin had been arrested, she again needed to bail him out of jail. She had seen the look before and this wasn't it. As the death notification of Collin Donovan Jackson was given to her by the officer, she screamed hysterically and reached for the phone knocking over the newly hand carved nativity scene her imprisoned son had made for her to call her husband a thousand miles away on a business trip.

The flight back to Louisiana from Atlanta was the longest flight Dale Jackson could ever recall. Deep down, he knew the extent of Collin's troubles and his chronic drug problems, but nothing could have prepared him for what he was about to face. He had watched his son be sentenced to a life in prison and the toll it had taken on his wife. He had witnessed the gruesome autopsy photographs of his once lively beautiful daughter in law, and had come to terms with her death and that his own son had caused it. Now, he would have to identify his dead grandson's body on a cold sterile table at the New Orleans city morgue amid the putrid stench of decomposed and mummified bodies that lie in wait to be fingerprinted and identified by homicide detectives.

Looking back, on the night of October 22, 2009, Collin believed he had found the girl of his dreams. She would become his family and his world. While Tracey Thibodeaux might not have had all the privileges of freedom that Collin Jackson had, she did have a stable home life. She grew up with her parents and older brother in an old historic home dating back to 1930 inherited by her great grandparents, Dr. John and Mrs. Caroline Latise, in Houma, Louisiana.

Once a sugar manor house, the old stately home situated on 6.1 acres is nestled amid oak, fruit and pecan trees. The original structure of the house maintained its Greek revival style of broad galleries and thick masonry walls, complimented by elaborate crown moldings, ornate cornices and ceiling medallions of a bygone era.

But for the installation of new wiring and plumbing, the Thibodeauxs had done little to restore the mansion that has frequently appeared in Houma's parade of homes over the course of several years.

The Thibodeaux's

Cherye Chalinor Latise Thibodeaux was one of seven children considered to be her grandmother's favorite. Unlike her other grandchildren, her granddaughter Helene found Cherye to have exemplary manners and a sense of appreciation and loyalty that she couldn't seem to identify with in her other grandchildren. When she became gravely ill, she summoned her lawyer to change her will so that when Cherye's mother died, she would be the designated golden child who would inherit the stately, historic mansion and all of its finest possessions.

Cherye Latise met Dirk Thibodeaux on a hot summer day at Lake Mary in Houma. While Dirk didn't grow up in a privileged family with old money like Cherye, he was a handsome, rugged man, who made her laugh and proved to be an honest, dependable, hardworking man. After a two-year courtship, the couple decided to marry and moved into her grandmother's mansion. Cherye's new husband was eager to fill up all the extra space with lots of children, but after two miscarriages, Cherye was content after the birth of their two children, Tim & Tracey.

Growing up in the 10-bedroom home for Tracey and Tim was an adventure. With a lively, large crew of cousins visiting for the holidays there was rarely a dull moment when the large historic home transformed into a grand hotel with many rooms and luxurious playground.

While the children would join the adults for holiday dinner in the formal dining room, the real adventures took place in the attic on the third floor. Tim and Tracey would play hide and seek with their cousins in the musty attic where there was all sorts of old furniture to hide behind, and then venture out to the vast sugar cane fields of Houma to continue the game of hide and seek.

Cajun City

Houma is a unique city 43 miles from the city of New Orleans, renowned for its hot spicy Cajun food, fishing, swamps, and southern hospitality. Most residents earn their income as shrimpers, oysterman, crabbers and fishermen. Houma is also known for its hurricane activity. On September 1, 2008, Houma was one of 34 Louisiana parishes affected by Hurricane Gustav, the second most destructive hurricane of the 2008 hurricane Atlantic season. Houma got the brunt of the storm and thousands of trees were uprooted, businesses were closed, and the rooftops of many homes in Houma were blown away. Much of the region was left without power. Tracey's family was fortunate. Other than downed trees and a lack of temporary power outage, the Thibodeaux's old house somehow withstood the wrath of the storm.

After the aftermath of Hurricane Gustav, the Thibodeaux's family life resumed to its regular routine. When Tracey's father Dirk was not working offshore in the oil field at the break of dawn he would set out to Bayou Sorrel and lower his fishing net among a cloud of pesky mosquitoes and gnats and wait for the bayou's powerful tide to float in a treasure chest of big juicy shrimp. On a good day he could catch 800 pounds of shrimp and sell it for $1 to $4 a pound, while Tracey's mother Cherye worked as the owner and curator of an elite antique store and museum in downtown Houma.

Collin And Tracey

In the small town of Houma, there's not a lot of stuff for teenagers to get into but Tracey, her friends and her brother, Tim, always seemed to find something to do. A lot of the local teenagers often met at 'The Mag' near Shrimper's Row where everybody knows everybody, so when the tall, mysterious teenager sporting a tattoo of a dark haired woman on his forearm seemingly appeared out of nowhere, he immediately stuck out like a sore thumb. Tracey Thibodeaux was instantly attracted to him. Always the over protective big brother, Tim immediately became suspicious and wondered about the strange guy his sister had taken an interest in. His name was Collin Jackson. He was hanging out with Hank Matherne, a local troublemaker, and he immediately sensed Collin was bad news. He also didn't seem like the type of guy Tim's parents would approve of and decided it was time to leave, but Tracey had already introduced herself to Collin and it didn't take long before the two lovebirds became inseparable. Tim suspected Collin was using drugs and warned his sister about him, but she blew off his comments while Collin had found himself a new girlfriend and a new home at the stately Thibodeaux residence.

Tim sensed a dark side about his sister's new boyfriend, always hanging around and often watched him and his sister argue when Collin was on his latest meth binge. He saw the bruises on his sister's arms, but she didn't seem to want to listen to anything her brother had to say. Tracey instead listened with an empathetic ear to Collin's tragic life circumstances over the loss of his father and mother, optimistic she could get him on the right track and they would live happily ever after.

On March 19, 2009, Tracey Thibodeaux's fairy tale ending came to an abrupt end. Instead of meeting up with her for lunch that day at the Mag, Collin never showed up. Instead, he skipped out on her and wasted another day high on Meth. Tracey had spoken to him throughout the day and knew he was off somewhere getting high again. Two days later when Collin showed up she told him she had enough and not to come around her house anymore, but Collin continued to show up unannounced anyway. Soon, the neighbors began to complain about the constant arguing between the acrimonious teenage couple and Tracey decided to finally break it off with him for good. But her words fell on deaf ears and Collin continued to remain a sinister fixture in Tracey's life.

Marcy Searcy lived a few houses down from the Thibodeauxs and had often babysat Tracey and Tim when they were little. She knew the long hours their parents worked and when they weren't around, she often checked in on them. She recently noticed a big change in Tracey upon meeting her new boyfriend. She was no longer worried, but afraid for Cherye Thibodeaux's daughter and alerted her mother about the boy who she said, "was up to no good."

Cherye started to work less hours after she discovered how badly things had gone south around the family home while she was away at work. Frustrated and worried about Tracey's troubled boyfriend hanging around her house, she had a long talk with her daughter about ending her relationship with him and told her he was no longer welcome at their home. Deep down, Tracey knew it was for the best but she still had feelings for Collin and started to sneak around against her mother's wishes and see him anyway. She joined him at parties rampant with dirty, disheveled meth and heroin addicts in seedy motels rooms with hundreds of needles lined up like toy soldiers on old dirty furniture. Collin would often become violent while under the influence of a vicious cocktail of drugs and Tracey would return home with swollen eyes and black and blue bruises covering her arms. Staring back at the girl in the mirror she could hardly recognize, she finally decided her relationship with Collin was over for good. But, Collin continued to stalk her wherever she would go and continue to show up at the Thibodeaux residence where arguments would routinely ensue between Tracey and her mother. By now, the cops had started to make routine visits out to the Thibodeaux residence, and since Tracey's father had sustained a serious back injury while falling off an oil rig, he was often confined to a bed under heavy sedation, not realizing what hell had descended within his once tranquil home. Things continued to deteriorate around the Thibodeaux residence and despite filing a restraining order, Collin Jackson remained undeterred.

On November 1, 2009, he again showed up in the middle of the night at the Thibodeaux residence and demanded Tracey leave with him. Tracey refused. The familiar sounds of arguing awakened Tim, who had long ago lost his patience with Collin. He ordered him out of the house and threatened to call the police but Collin ignored him and seemed unfazed by Tim's threats. Tracey's mother also awakened to the commotion, stunned to see Collin standing in her living room at such a late hour demanding that her daughter leave with him. Outraged, she too threatened to call the police once again but when her words, too, fell on deaf ears, she told her son to go and get the gun. Hopefully, this would scare him off for good. Tim didn't hesitate. He had long ago been fed up with Collin Jackson and made his way down the darkness of the long hallway to his parents' bedroom and grabbed the .357 magnum from his father's nightstand drawer. When he returned to the living room, to his left, he saw his father's collection of native and cowboy embellishments scattered about the room and a dramatic Indian portrait splashed in red lying on the floor. To his right, he found his mother and sister lying motionless on the old pine plank floors beaten beyond recognition. His mind could not take in the horrific scene of what he was seeing. Like an actor playing a part in a horror flick, he turned to Collin Jackson standing across the room and released the trigger, firing three shots into the right temple of Collin Jackson. Within seconds, the explosive sounds of the .357 magnum resonated throughout the old house where Collin Jackson's body fell on an old antique trestle table.

For Theresa Searcy sleep never came easy and she once again found herself up again tossing and turning throughout the night. She always left the TV on when she went to bed but on this particular night she needed to get a good night's rest for an important meeting at work the next day, and so she decided to turn it off. Just as the bright red digital numbers on her alarm clock flickered to 2:05 a.m., she finally dozed off only to be jolted out of her sleep at the explosive sounds of gun shots. She dialed 911 and instinctively ran to the Thibodeaux residence.

Deputy Walt Hill of the Houma Police Department was at the scene of a car wreck on 420 St. Joseph Street when he got the call, "Man Down" at the old sugar manor house. He met with Fire Chief Darryl Newhouse. They had already strung the crime scene tape around the Thibodeaux residence. EMS arrived and minutes later paramedics lifted the small framed woman in her forties and young girl about 18 in to the ambulance. The older woman was conscience and hysterical, while the young girl remained unconscious and motionless. He observed the broken jaw the young girl had sustained and the gruesome nature of injuries to her nose displaced to the right side of her face, and knew that it would take several surgeries to reconstruct the trauma to her face wrought upon her by her attacker.

As Sergeant Hill entered the Thibodeaux residence, he could see the dead man lying on his right side on the top of an antique table in the family living room. A young man about 20 stood nearby in a catatonic-like state. He gave his name as Tim Thibodeaux. A woman standing next to him introduced herself to the officer as Theresa Searcy, a family friend and neighbor. She directed officers to the back room where Dirk Thibodeaux, the man of the house, remained in a deep sleep under the influence of several narcotics his doctors had prescribed to him to ease the pain that had riddled his body since falling off the oil rig he had been working on last summer. Eventually, he would wake up to a nightmare.

Sergeant Milton Mahoney had been dispatched to the scene a quarter after three. He and Hill slipped on latex gloves and crossed the yellow tape walking towards the dead man's body. There was blood splatter from the deceased covering the walls and drops of blood and smudges on the furniture and carpet in the family room. Mahoney spotted 4 spent bullet casings that had rolled under a sofa table in the center of the room. Hill and Mahoney were eager to talk with Tim Thibodeaux at the police station but it was almost 5:00 a.m. until Detectives Frank Sloan and Robert Myers had bagged all the physical evidence.

Dr. Charles Reynaud, associate medical examiner for Terrebonne Parish, was called to the scene too. After Collin Jackson's body was photographed and then removed for autopsy, Hill and Mahoney took Tim Thibodeaux into custody and headed down to the police station to interview him.

The small town of Houma was ablaze with rumors. No one knew at that point who had killed the mysterious young man frequently seen at the Thibodeaux residence. When detectives phoned Collin Jackson's grandfather to notify him his grandson had been murdered, Stan Colton broke down in tears. His wife Laurel was still asleep and he could not bear to wake her to deliver the horrible news. "Was he shot by a drug dealer?" he asked the detective. I have always imagined that would happen to him. He had a big problem with drugs." "Sir, we have a suspect and he has been brought into police custody," the officer said. We will be in contact with you as soon as we have completed our investigation." Stan Colton wouldn't have to deliver the horrific news to his wife. She had already heard it all on the other end of the phone line in the house. As she walked towards Stan sitting in the dark family room with the blinds drawn yielding a glimmer of early morning light, she stared at him blankly and didn't utter a word.

The next 72 hours passed in a blur for both of Collin Jackson's grandparents, relatives and friends. His fatal shooting made the top of television news and newspaper headlines. For those who never forgot the story of the little boy who watched in horror as his father fatally shot his mother and then turned the gun on himself, they were shocked and grief- stricken. While they didn't know the events that precipitated his murder, or the extent of Collin's drug problems, they still thought of him as him as the lost five-year old little boy without parents. Before he became hooked on drugs, he had made it his mission to free his father from the walls of prison so they could be a family again. In a sad twisted irony, he blamed the drugs that altered his father's behavior causing the murder of his mother, and then lost his own life because of the altered behavior of the drugs that he himself abused.

Down at the Houma police department, detectives believed this was going to be a slam-dunk case. Yes, he had been at the scene of the crime and yes he discovered his mother and sister brutally beaten, but, no, he had not killed Collin Jackson. He arrived home to find his mother and sister beaten beyond recognition. Detectives weren't buying it. Armed with so much forensic evidence, Simone Stanson, a senior deputy prosecution attorney for Terrebonne Parish, filed an affidavit of arrest for Tim

Derek Thibodeaux on second degree murder charges and it was granted. Judge Hilton Guidry set Tim's bail at $500,000. While the Terrebonne Parish detectives knew Collin Jackson had been shot with .357 magnum, the question was where was the gun?

Gordon Ellis' phone rang just as he was calling it a day. Ellis had made a reputation for himself as a successful criminal defense attorney in the town of Houma and its surrounding parishes, but he was about to turn 65 and ready to close shop and retire. He groaned as he begrudgingly picked up the phone that wouldn't stop ringing so he could go home and pour himself a stiff gin and tonic. At the other end of the line he heard a frantic woman's voice. Her name was Theresa Searcy, pouring out her story, her words tripping over one another. It was a hell of a story, but not one that would shock Ellis in his 30 years of law practice. In all of his years of defending hardened criminals, there wasn't much that could get past Ellis. He had heard it all.

"Tim was at my house tonight," Theresa Searcy said. "Did you tell the police that?" asked Ellis. "Yes," she said. Elllis contacted the district attorney and Tim Thibodeaux was released on a 20,000 bond. As investigators continued to search for the gun and for any evidence linking Tim Thibodeaux to the crime, there just didn't seemed to be any. There was no weapon or solid physical evidence that might incriminate Tim Thibodeaux that would be strong enough to present to the prosecutor. His most powerful defense was his alibi. As investigators pushed Tim to come back in for another interrogation and a polygraph, they hit a wall when they learned he had lawyered up. Gordon Ellis had taken over now and the boy couldn't be touched. They were now confident Tim Thibodeaux was involved in the murder of Collin Jackson. Seasoned homicide detectives like Hill and Mahoney knew that that the innocent usually talked and the guilty lawyered up and walked. The hunt was on for the murder weapon as Cherye and Tracey Thibodeaux spent weeks in the hospital undergoing surgeries and recovering from their injuries.

After detectives visited with the Coltons and heard all about their troubled grandson's life story, a clear picture of Collin Jackson emerged. Means, motive and opportunity were all reasons for Tim Thibodeaux to shoot him. But, after months of searching for the weapon, detectives had hit a wall so they paid a visit to Theresa Searcy who Tim claimed he had been with at the time of the murder. Again, she corroborated his alibi.

Downtown back at the police station Mahoney was not convinced that Searcy was telling them all she knew.

She was a neighbor but nothing more. She seemed to live a solitary life and had worked in human resources for a local bottling company for several years. Co-workers and those who knew her all had positive things to say about her. Others whom she didn't work with didn't really know much about her and told detectives that she generally kept to herself.

As Cherye Thibodeaux recovered from her injuries and returned home, detectives set up surveillance. Theresa Searcy could often be observed visiting the Thibodeaux residence, bringing food over, but then detectives noticed an interesting pattern. She was often there when Tim was there and Cherye wasn't.

While Tim couldn't be touched under the legal protection of Gordon Ellis, Theresa Searcy could, and so detectives became a daily fixture of Theresa's comings and goings. Wherever she went, detectives were never far behind. Meanwhile, Tim had become a shell of himself. He hardly ate, slept and often skipped school. He was there for each of his sister's surgeries. She miraculously survived the vicious beating and was allowed to go home after spending two months in the hospital. The Thibodeauxs clung together and remained tight-lipped through it all. They shied away from pesky reporters' questions and refused to give television interviews about the horrid ordeal. They had no memory of it and had nothing to share with the media.

On the outside, Tim Thibodeaux strived hard to resume an ordinary life, but on the inside it was eating him alive. After several failed suicide attempts, on January 23, 2010 he called the Houma Police Station and asked to speak to one of the lead detectives on the case. Mahoney had been with the department for 15 years and had seen his share of troubled souls, but none like Tim Thibodeaux. As the skinny, disheveled teenager approached him, he could see the look of defeat in his eyes. "I shot Collin Jackson," he said. And there it was. Detective Mahoney immediately grabbed his tape recorder and shut the door to the interrogation room. Thibodeaux didn't want to speak to anyone else and said he would end the confession if anyone else was present. Mahoney honored his wishes and listened intently as Tim Thibodeaux released the ugly secret that had held him hostage for a year. He confessed to killing Collin Jackson and told the detective how he found his mother and sister viciously beaten by him. With a guilty plea bargain under the advice of his attorney, Tim Thibodeaux waived a jury trial and was charged and convicted of manslaughter. He was sentenced to serve a 20- year life sentence without the benefit of parole at the Louisiana State Penitentiary where Collin Jackson's father continues to serve life imprisonment for his mother's murder. Theresa Searcy is now serving 15 years for obstruction of justice at St. Gabriel Women's Prison.